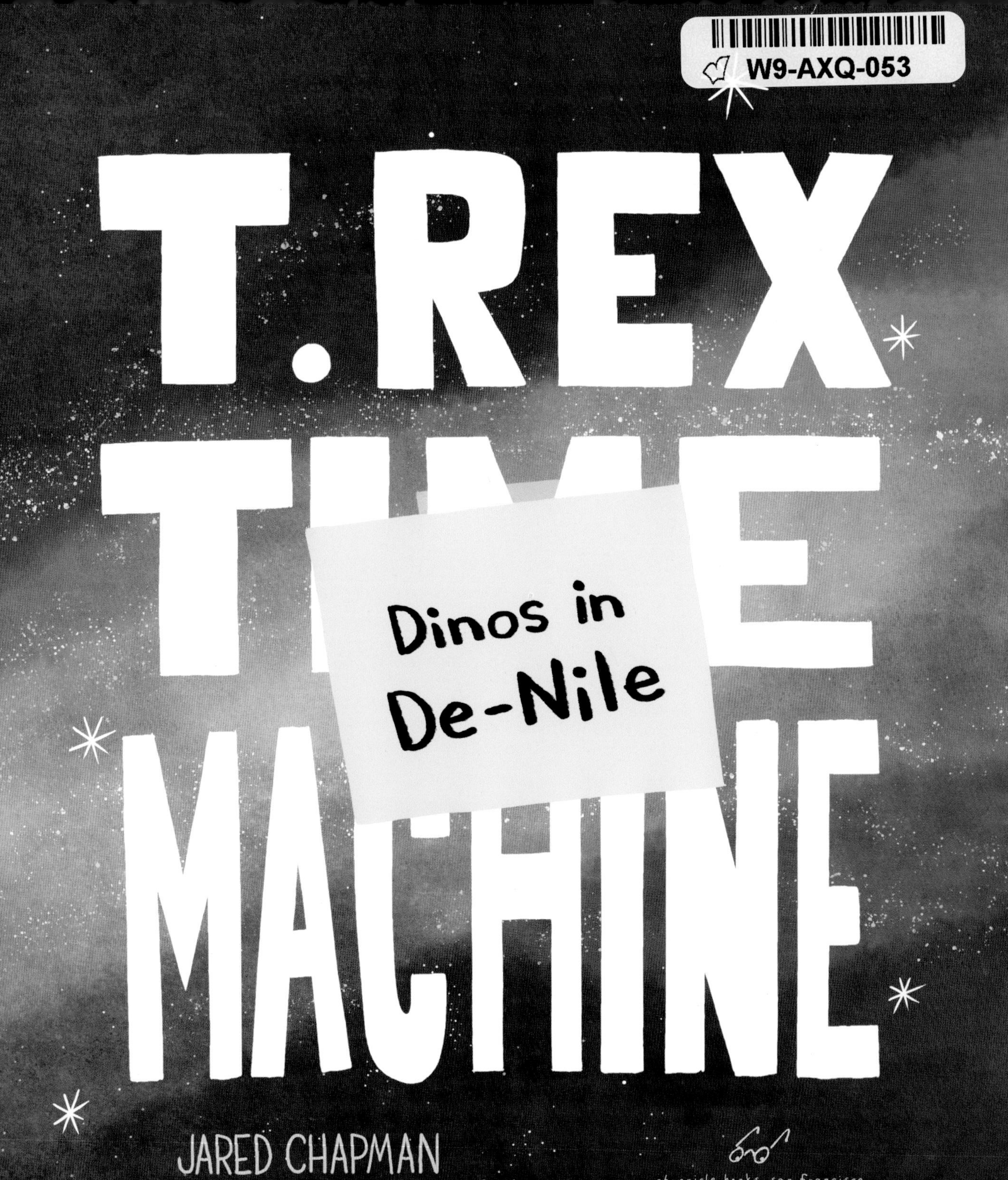

W9-AXQ-053
T. REX
TIME
MACHINE
Dinos in
De-Nile
JARED CHAPMAN
chronicle books · san francisco

One day two dinosaurs escaped from danger on a time machine and hurtled to a far off land . . .

Didn't do it!

. . . with very hot sand.

So they quickly set off to find more habitable conditions.

Ahhh!
Finally.

Ack! Squish it!
Snap!
Snap!

A boat passing nearby saw the dinosaurs.

You there! Halt!

The pharaoh would like a word with you.

SOBEK!
Pharaoh?

Sobek! I'm Tut, and I am such a fan! I've read all your comic books! Your posters are all over my palace walls!
Who's Sobek?

Ha ha! I had no idea that the god of the Nile would be so funny. I'm so thrilled you're here. Please allow me to throw a feast in your honor.
Um . . . ok?
Yay! We're staying for dinner!

Later that night, the dinosaurs were celebrated.

Egypt is pretty great.
I'm so glad you think so, Sobek.
My mouth is empty! Feed me!

It would be my honor to show you my kingdom.
What? There's more?

The next day, the dinosaurs were given a tour.
This is our lighthouse.

Library of Alexandria
And this is where
I check out all
your comic books.

And this is the Nile River, but I guess you already knew that, right? Get it? You're the god of this river.
Yes, I got it.

And this was a practical joke that got out of hand.

Who are they?
Oh, them? Those are the aliens.

They come down every couple of weeks to work on that triangle project.
We've never seen those things before and absolutely **DID NOT** crash into one.

Just then, the aliens noticed the dinosaurs.

HEY, LOOK!

What's wrong, Marty?

Dinosaurs! I bet they did it!

The aliens explained how the dinosaurs became extinct millions of years before . . .

Dinosaurs?!

Extinct?!

. . . and that a time machine had recently crashed into the latest addition to their triangle project, destroying it.

Was this revenge for the meteor? That was an accident!

Ha ha! Dinosaurs? Good one, but we're actually gods, right, Tut, ol' buddy?

And unfortunately, the aliens had terrible timing.

Tut was hurt and embarrassed.

You're not gods?
How could you lie
to me like that?

Then he got mad.

Guards, arrest these . . .
DINOSAURS!

That'll teach you to
smash an alien's work!

Back on the boat,
Tut decided the dinosaurs' fate.

The dinosaurs looked around for a way to escape.

Ack! Squish them again!
Guards, after them!
SWIM!

SOMETHING JUST BIT MY TOES!
GET OFF ME!

RUN! NOW!
I TOLD YOU! I TOLD YOU!

The dinosaurs had to get out of
Ancient Egypt fast.

Hot! Hot! Hot!
My feet feel great.
Squeak
Squeak
Squeak

And what do two creatures from the Mesozoic Era know about future technology?

Drag them out...

...and take them back to the boat!
Boat? You got it!

Well, that didn't end well.

Things can only
get better, right?

For Rebecca Sherman.

Library of Congress Cataloging-in-Publication Data available.

ISBN 978-1-4521-6155-6

Manufactured in China.

Design by Ryan Hayes and Julia Marvel.
Lettering by Jared Chapman.
Typeset in Coop Forged.
The illustrations for this book were originally done with ink of papyrus. It was a big hassle. Luckily, an alien on his lunch break saw the author struggling and suggested recreating everything digitally in Photoshop. Alien technology sometimes gets a bad rap, but in this case, it worked out really well. The aliens refused to give the author a ride in their spaceship, thus ending their working relationship.

10 9 8 7 6 5 4 3 2 1

Chronicle Books LLC
680 Second Street
San Francisco, California 94107

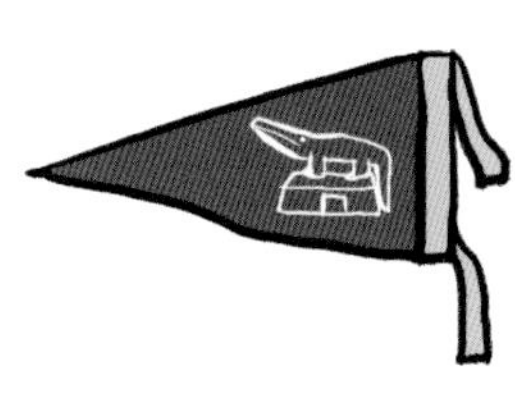